RM. 201

THE STUDY GROUP

BY KELLY ROGERS
ILLUSTRATED BY BETSY PETERSCHMIDT

Spellbound

An Imprint of Magic Wagon
abdopublishing.com

For Aida, My kind and thoughtful girl,
who always takes the cheese off her pizza. —KRP

To Erika and Hayley: for all the sleepovers
we spent laughing until dawn. —BP

abdopublishing.com

Published by Magic Wagon, a division of ABDO, PO Box 398166, Minneapolis, Minnesota 55439. Copyright © 2017 by Abdo Consulting Group, Inc. International copyrights reserved in all countries. No part of this book may be reproduced in any form without written permission from the publisher. Spellbound™ is a trademark and logo of Magic Wagon.

Printed in the United States of America, North Mankato, Minnesota.
052016
092016

THIS BOOK CONTAINS
RECYCLED MATERIALS

Written by Kelly Rogers
Illustrated by Betsy Peterschmidt
Edited by Heidi M.D. Elston and Megan M. Gunderson
Designed by Candice Keimig

Library of Congress Cataloging-in-Publication Data
Names: Rogers, Kelly, 1981- author. | Peterschmidt, Betsy, illustrator.
Title: Study group / by Kelly Rogers ; illustrated by Betsy Peterschmidt.
Description: Minneapolis, MN : Magic Wagon, [2017] | Series: Rm. 201 |
    Summary: Neesha's friend Amy has been behaving very strangely since she joined
    Ms. Fleek's study group, ever so well behaved but remote--but Neesha misses her
    friend so much that she joins the group too, and immediately feels a change
    coming over her.
Identifiers: LCCN 2016002315 (print) | LCCN 2016005466 (ebook) | ISBN
    9781624021701 (lib. bdg.) | ISBN 9781680790498 (ebook)
Subjects: LCSH: Horror tales. | Science teachers--Juvenile fiction. | Middle
    schools--Juvenile fiction. | CYAC: Horror stories. | Teachers--Fiction. |
    Middle schools--Fiction. | Schools--Fiction.
Classification: LCC PZ7.1.R65 St 2016 (print) | LCC PZ7.1.R65 (ebook) | DDC
    813.6--dc23
LC record available at http://lccn.loc.gov/2016002315

TABLE OF CONTENTS

CHAPTER 1
Neesha Can Wait . . . 4

CHAPTER 2
Sleeping . . . 14

CHAPTER 3
A Rough Week . . . 24

CHAPTER 4
Welcome Neesha . . . 36

CHAPTER 1
Neesha Can Wait

Ms. Fleek is alone in her room. It is late. The only LIGHT comes from the computer. Her *eyes* scan left and right across the screen. She is looking at the names of students. She is looking for just the right ones.

"Neesha Ahmed," she *mutters*. "Not yet. Grades too high." Her eyes scan further down the list. "Marcus Bunt? Maybe." She looks harder. "F in math. No."

Then Ms. Fleek's face lights up with a **GRIN**. "Bs in most classes, just one C in gym. Perfect."

Ms. Fleek picks up her *pen*.
She writes a name on the envelope
in front of her. She puts it on top of
a tall pile of invitations.
"**WELCOME** to my
study group," says
Ms. Fleek.

AMY VANG

"Hey Amy!" I called. Amy stopped just outside of Ms. Fleek's CLASSROOM. She turned and waved at me. But she didn't smile.

"Uh," I began. I hadn't really thought she would STOP. "Want to come to my house after school?"

When Amy joined Ms. Fleek's study group, she stopped sitting with me at lunch. She got really quiet.

Amy also started getting As in every class. It only took her two weeks! Ms. Fleek is kind of strange, but that must be some group.

Amy still had not answered. She just stood there. I tried one more thing. "You can sleep over?"

Amy **looked** into RM. 201.

I could see Ms. Fleek inside her classroom. *Did Ms. Fleek just nod her head?*

Amy turned back to me. This time she smiled. "Okay, Neesha," she said. "I'll come over after study group."

CHAPTER 2

Sleeping

Amy showed up at dinnertime. I had spent **forever** getting ready. I had all the usual *sleepover* things: popcorn, brownies, and a stack of movies. Mom had ordered an extra large, extra cheese pizza.

I almost **BOUNCED** when Amy came into the kitchen.

"Come eat!" I said.

Amy looked at the table.

She made a face like she was

smelling garbage instead of pizza.

16

"No, thank you," Amy said. "I ate at study group."

Amy didn't **eat** the brownies or popcorn either! I did. Because that's what sleepovers are for. But nothing TASTED the same.

At least Amy said yes to
everything else.

"Do you want to play cards?"
I asked.

"Sure," said Amy.

"Should we paint our nails?"

"Sure," said Amy.

But a few hours later, I ran out
of questions. I was really tired.

"Should we go to bed now?"

"Sure," said Amy.

I got my extra bed ready. Amy helped, but she didn't say much. We both climbed into our beds. It was so quiet. I fell asleep right away.

But I could not stay asleep. I tossed and turned. I looked at the clock. It was 2:12 a.m. I kept thinking about our strange night.

It was so different from other sleepovers! What if I hadn't come up with plans? Why wasn't Amy hungry? I looked over at Amy.

Amy was lying on her back.
Her eyes were OPEN, like she
was staring at the ceiling. She
didn't *blink* once.

CHAPTER 3

A Rough Week

"Everyone quiet down. **Now!**"

my math teacher said. Mr. Norbit

had been **MAD** all morning.

"These test scores are *TERRIBLE*!

Get your notebooks out. We're

having a pop quiz."

I sat working at my desk,

still and *quiet*.

There was no talking. There
was only the sound of pencil
SCRATCHING paper, of book
pages *turning* quietly.

Cesar had already been sent
out of the room for . . . well, I don't
know *why* he was sent out.

Mr. Norbit PATROLLED the aisles. He was looking for students who were off task.

I **STARED** at my paper. I did not even breathe loudly. Most of the other students did the same.

Only Amy and Griffin, a boy from the study group, were working *happily*.

Social studies was the **same**. I was behind in my group work. I still needed to **color** in my maps. My teacher handed out **MORE** work sheets. And there were *surprise* quizzes!

Even English, my favorite, was TERRIBLE. Ms. Martinez was normally nice and funny. I always look forward to her class.

Today, I was getting my essay back. I had worked so hard on it! It might not get an A, but it might get a B.

Ms. Martinez **frowned** when she handed me my essay. I was almost too scared to look. But there it was: a big, red C-. **C-!**

The last week had been so **HARD**! I had twice the homework as usual. I couldn't seem to catch up.

I *missed* the way school used to be. I *missed* Amy.

My whole life seemed turned upside down. I felt like *crying*.

At lunch, I walked by the table where I used to sit with Amy. She was with Griffin and some of the other study group kids.

I heard Griffin say, "I told that kid he should have joined the study group." Then the whole table laughed.

I sat at my new table in
the corner. ALONE. Mom had
made my favorite, egg salad. But I
didn't feel like eating. I didn't want
to go to the rest of my classes.

CHAPTER 4
Welcome Neesha

I was really grumpy by my last class. RM. 201. Science with Ms. Fleek.

Just before I walked in the door, Amy stopped me.

"Hi, Neesha!" Amy said. Her face was lit up by a bright smile. "Griffin and I wondered . . . do you want to come to study group today?"

I didn't really want to go. But it had been so long since Amy had invited me to anything.

"There will be pizza," Amy said. She **STARED** straight at me, not blinking, waiting.

Ms. Fleek was weird. But it had been a very hard week. And pizza sounded good.

"Okay," I said. I **tried** to smile.

Science turned into the **BEST** part of my day. I finished my work before the hour was over.

Ms. Fleek didn't smile, but Ms. Fleek never smiled.

Nobody got in *TROUBLE*.

Amy and Griffin even asked me to sit with them! Amy smiled and laughed the whole class.

When the **bell rang**, no one left Ms. Fleek's room. The whole class was staying for the study group pizza party.

Ms. Fleek went into her back room. It was marked NO STUDENTS EVER. When she came back, she was carrying five boxes of pizza. She locked the door behind her.

One of them was my favorite, extra cheese. It was flavored with some green sprinkles. *It must be an herb. Maybe oregano*, I thought. It was so good I ate three pieces.

When I went home that day,
I felt **strange**. But not
bad. I didn't feel like eating dinner.
I cleaned up my room without
being asked.

The next morning, I felt better than I had in weeks.

My mom put a plate of hash browns and scrambled eggs on the table. I WRINKLED my nose. "No thanks, Mom. I'm not hungry."

"Is everything *okay*? You didn't eat your dinner last night! And where is your smile?"

"Everything is GREAT!" I stood up and grabbed my bag. "I'll be late today, Mom, okay?"

"Oh, why's that?"

Then I did smile. For the first time since coming home yesterday. "I joined Ms. Fleek's study group."